ANASTASIA

A Don Bluth/Gary Goldman Film

PARTY WITH BARTOK!

A Division of HarperCollins*Publishers*

Copyright © 1998 by Twentieth Century Fox Film Corporation.
HarperCollins®, 📕®, and HarperActive are trademarks of HarperCollins Publishers Inc.
Printed in the U.S.A. All rights reserved.
ISBN: 0–06–107087–4
Written by Jennifer Alton and Cynthia A. Nason
Concept art by Len Simon
Illustrated by Fox Animation Studios
Art colorized by Dan and Tracy Smith
Special thanks to Mary H. Busacca

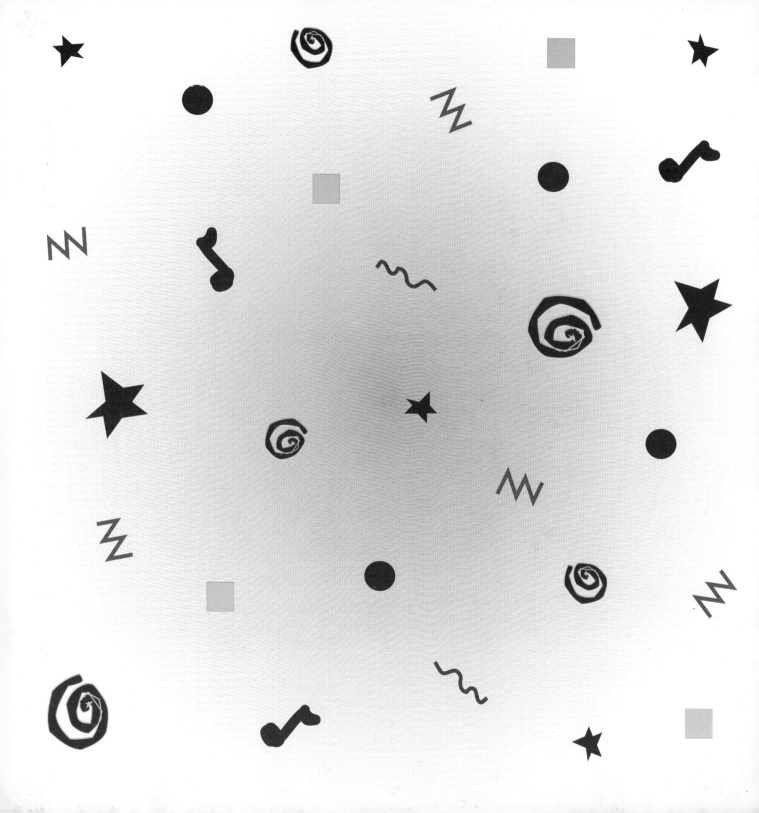

I hear you want to learn to dance.
A party's where you'll get your chance.

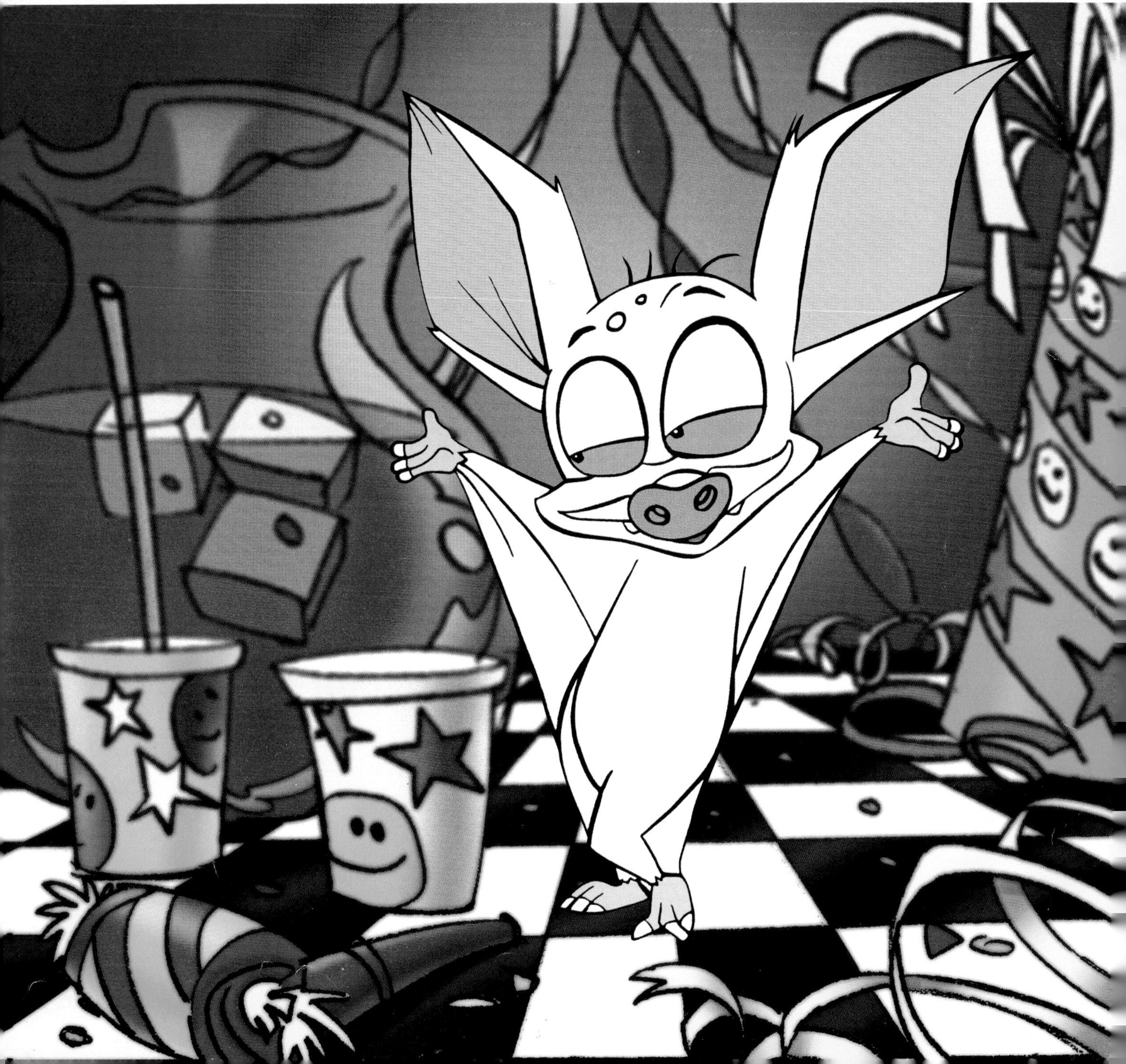

Come on with me. We'll do the rumba.

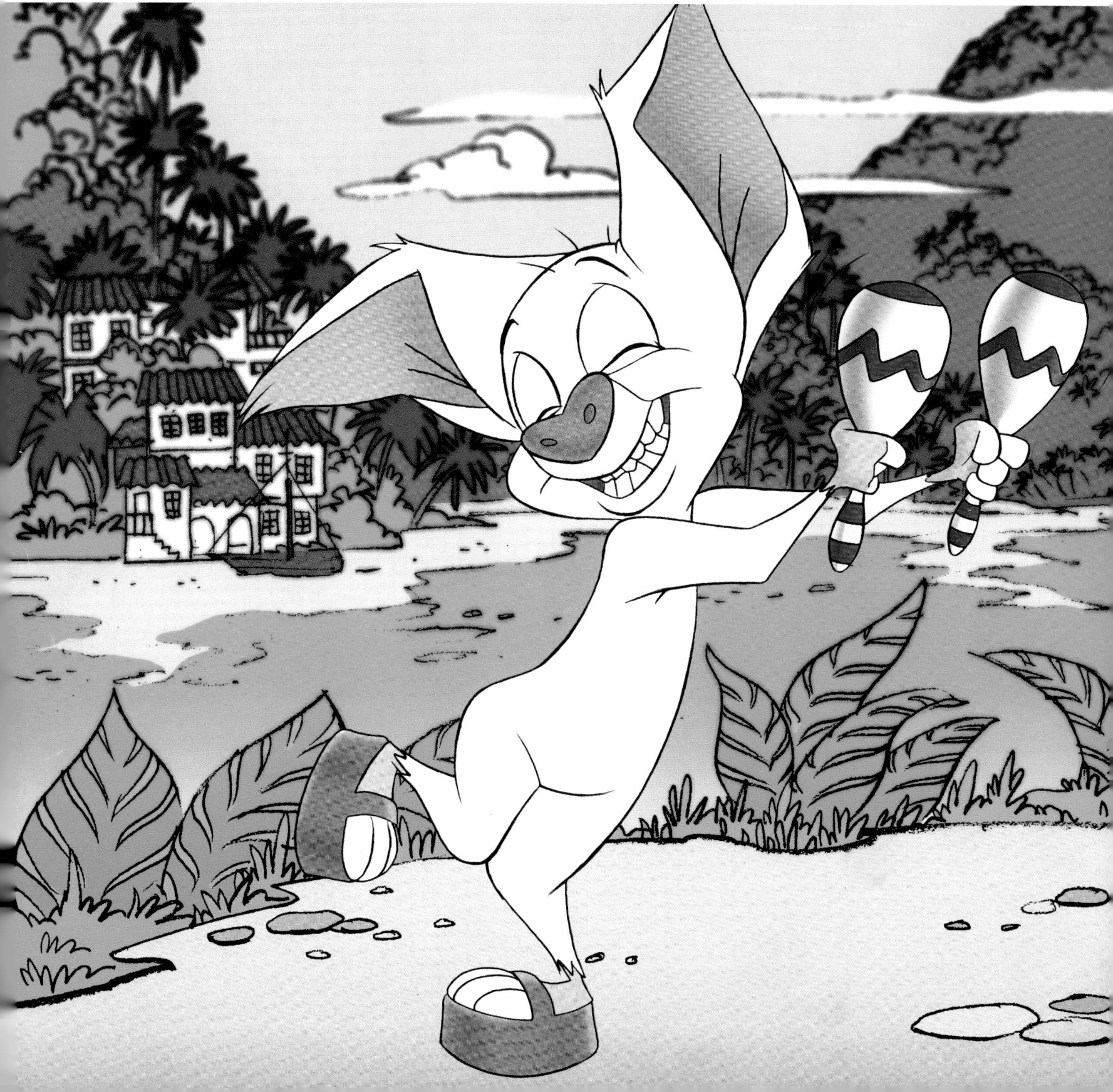

Not like that! *Ay caramba!*

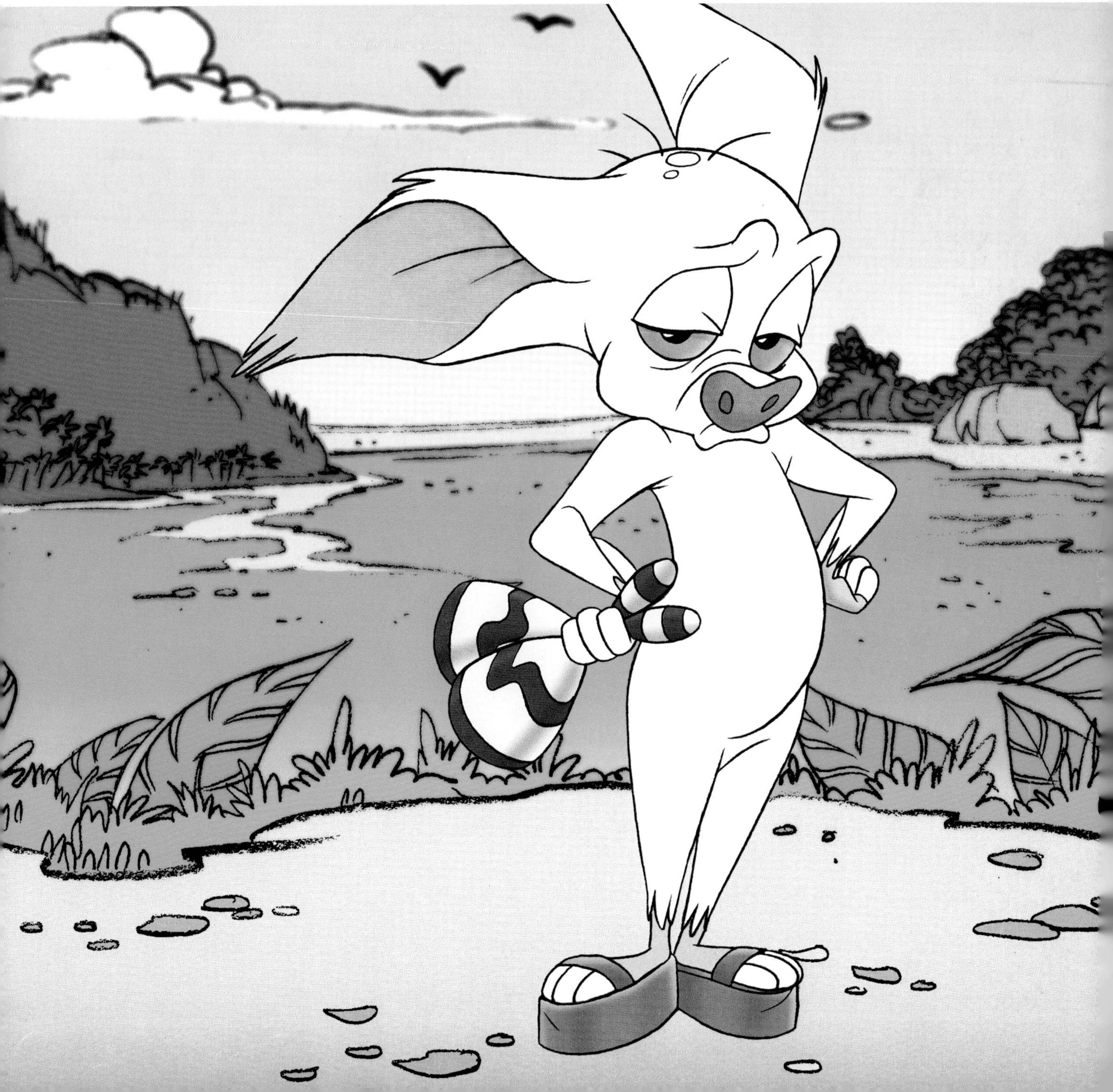

Let me show you how to tango,

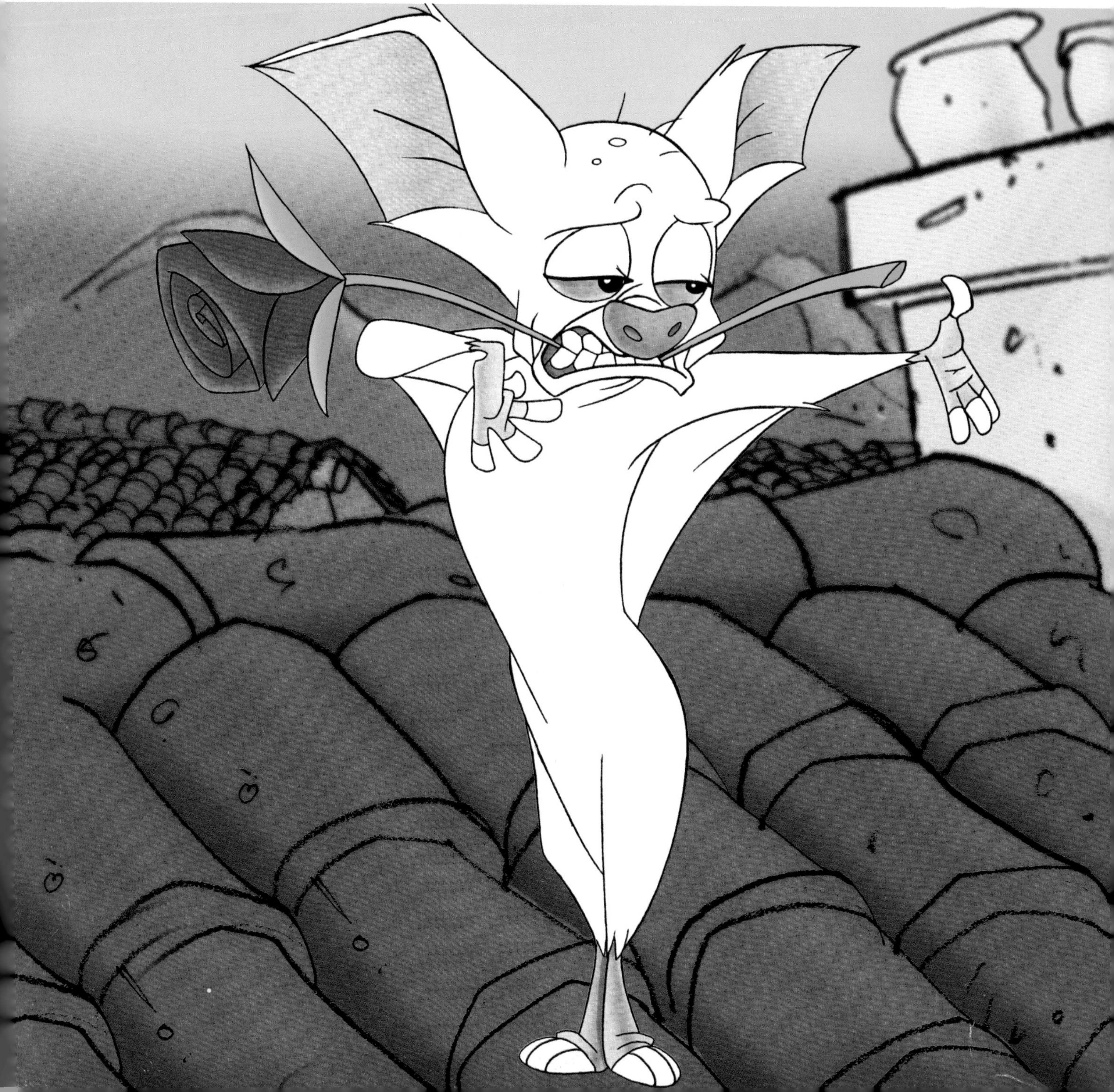

or do a little fast fandango.

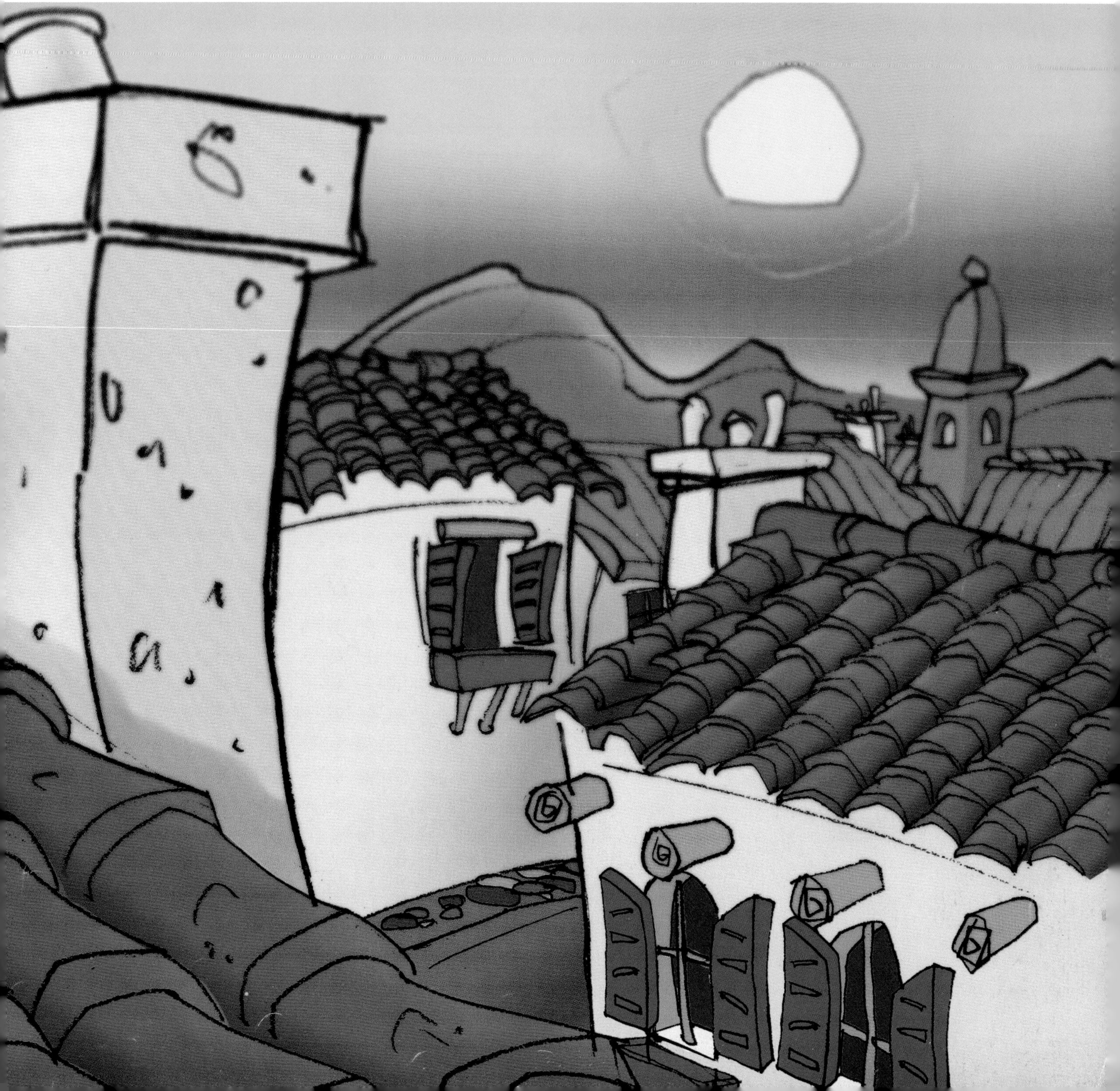

You could even learn to tap.

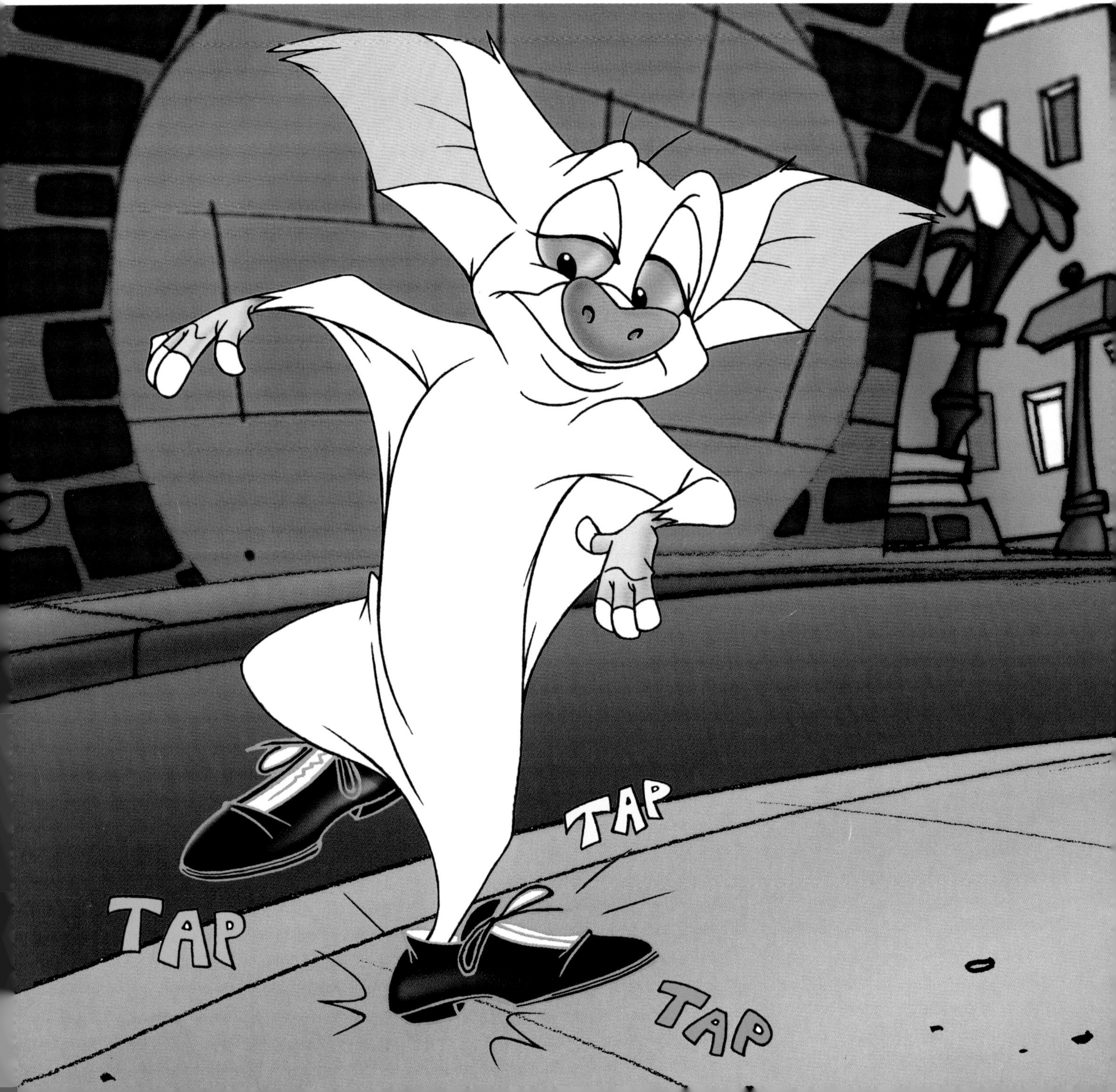
TAP
TAP
TAP

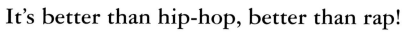

It's better than hip-hop, better than rap!

Disco and you may not be such a good thing.

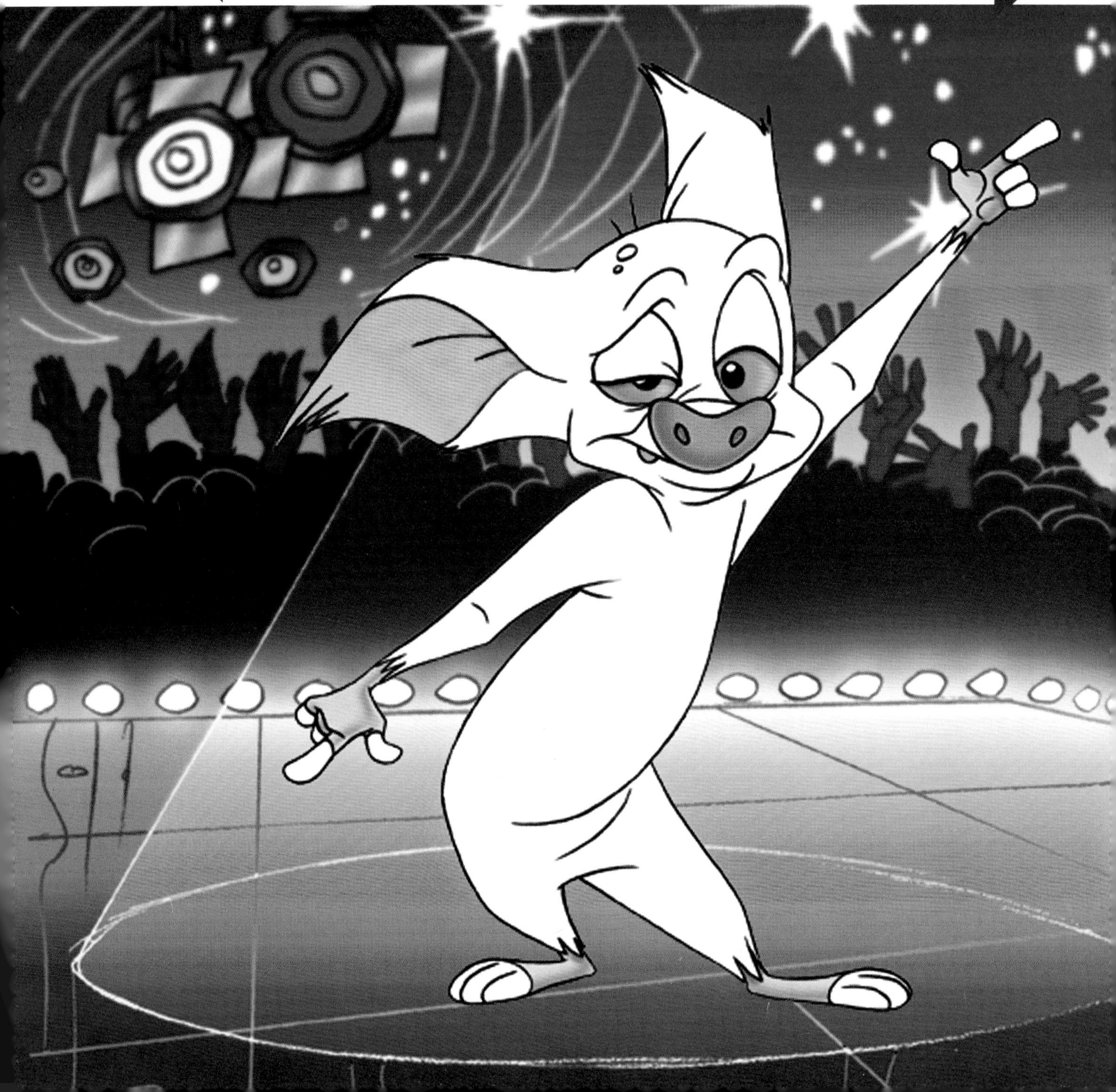

But watch me and learn. I'm the dance floor king!

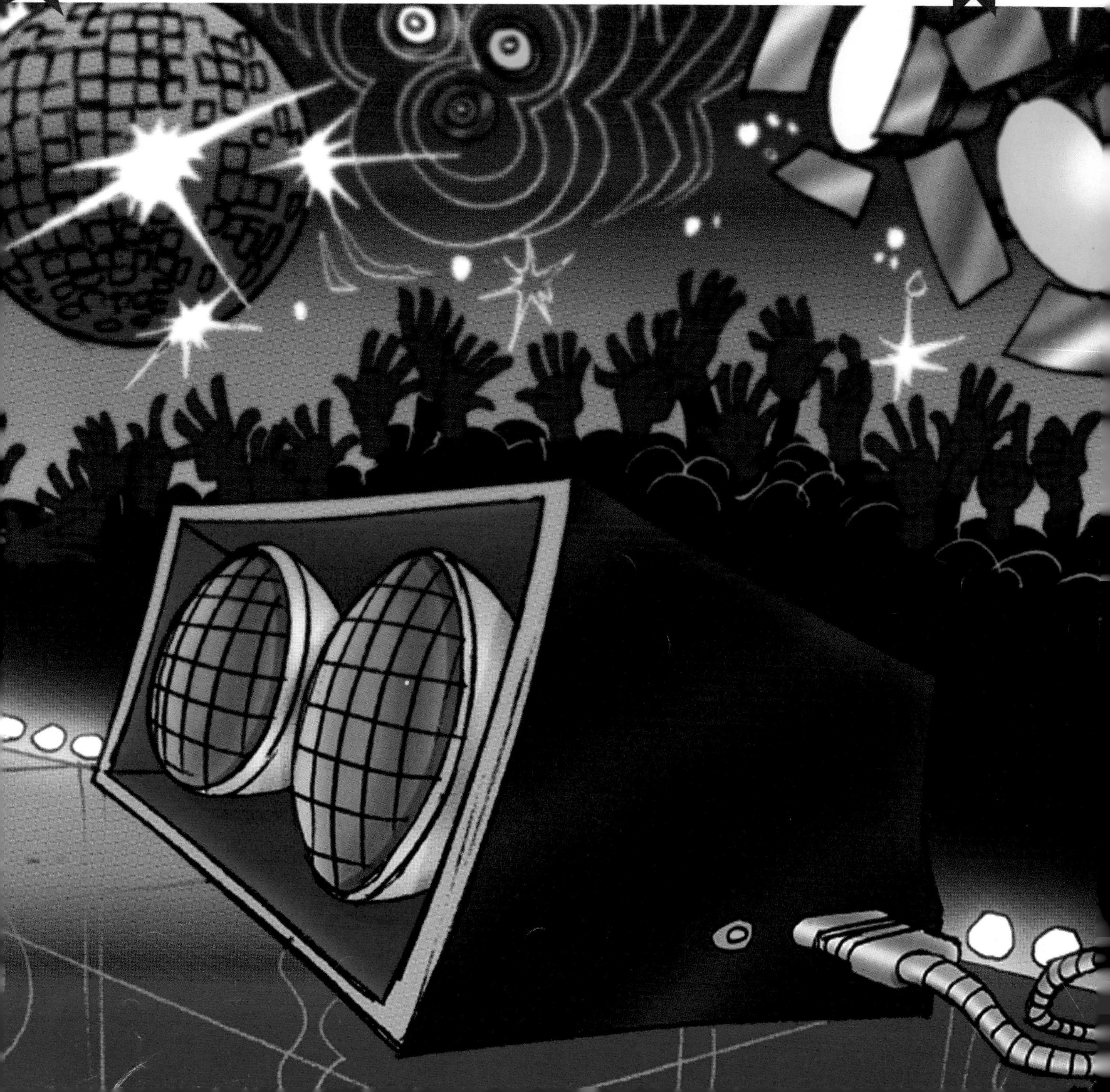

The line dance isn't all that easy.

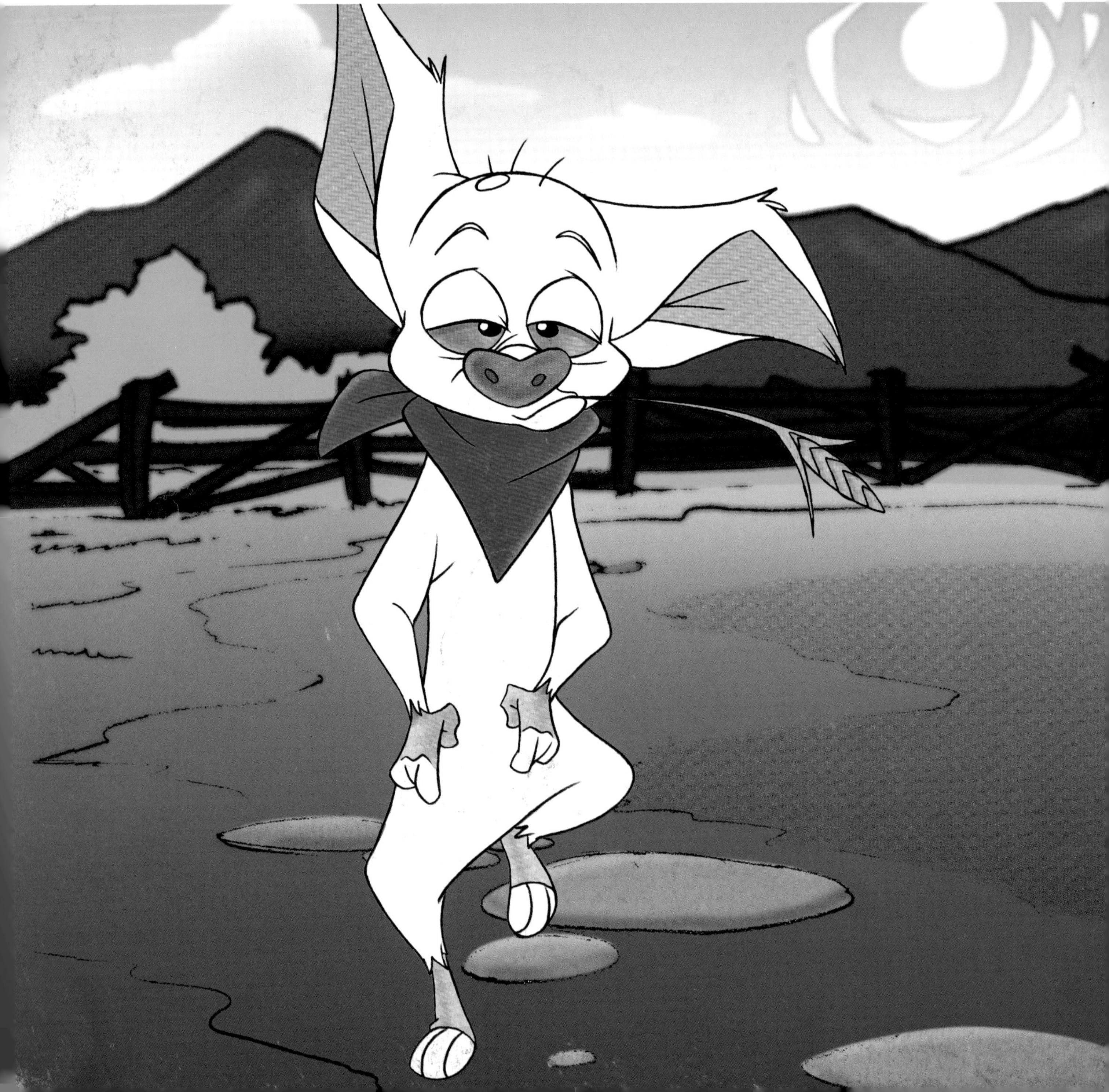

Hey, sometimes even *I* get queasy!

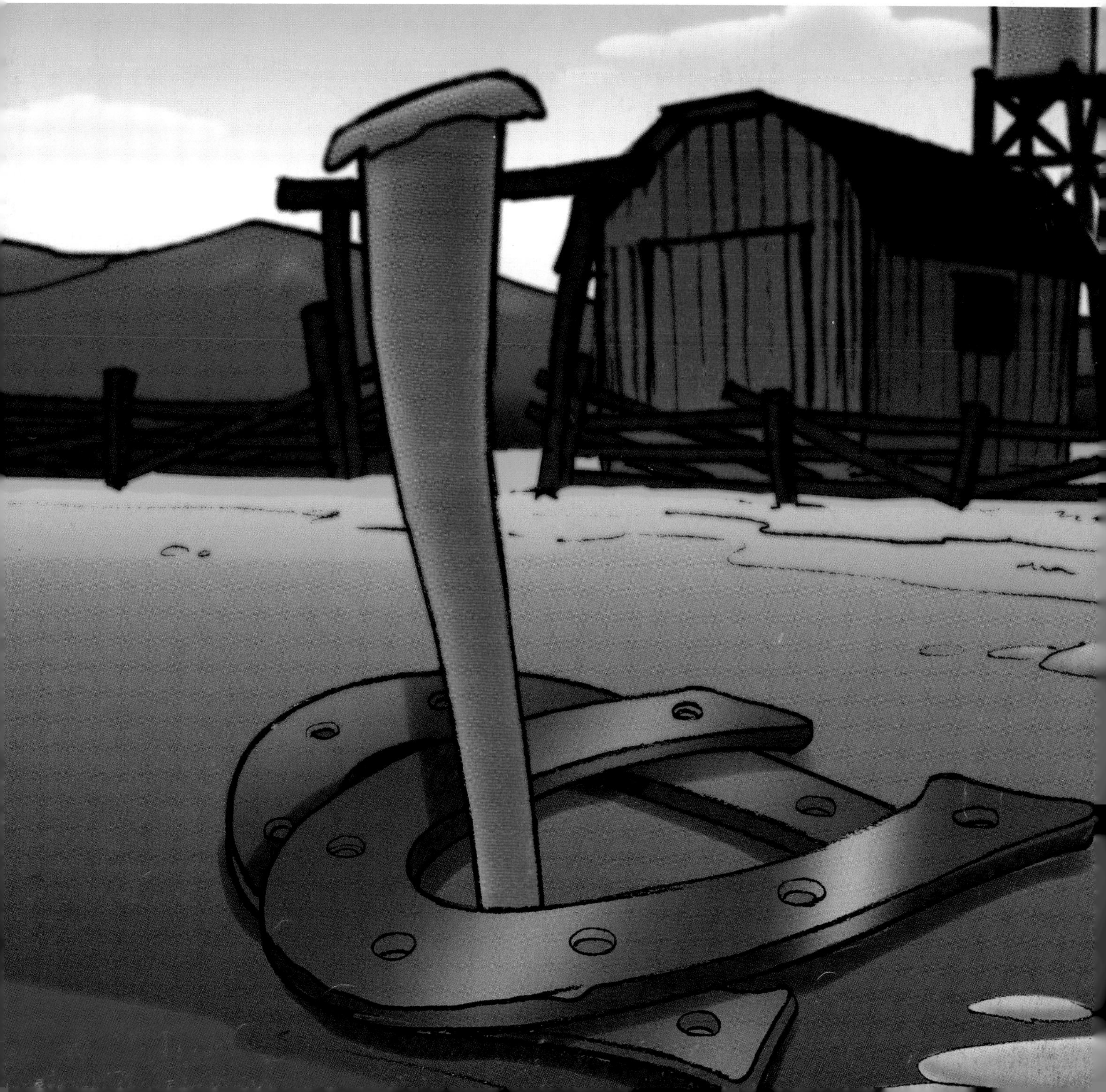

The dance for you is the jitterbug.

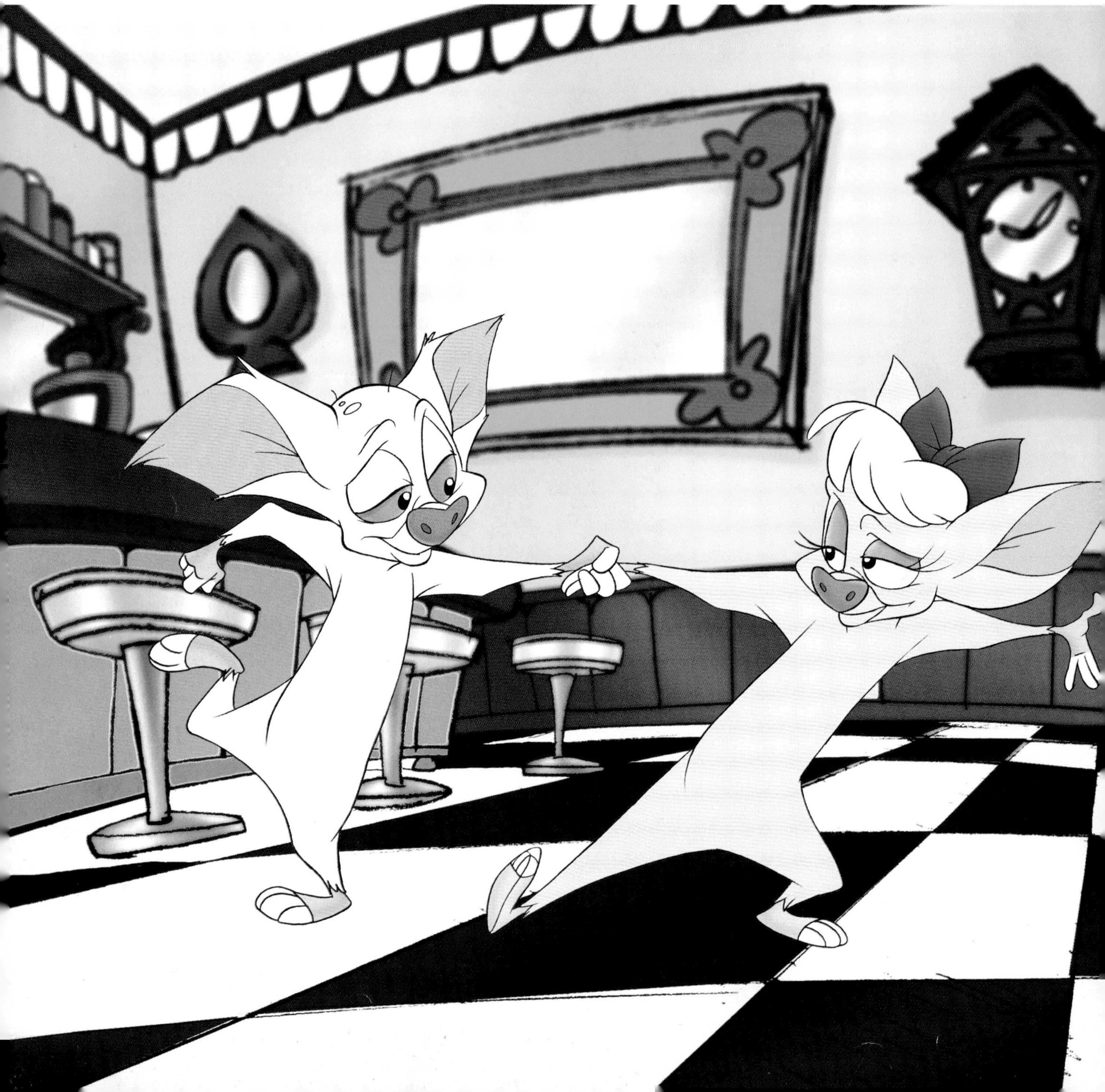

Now *this* is how you cut a rug!

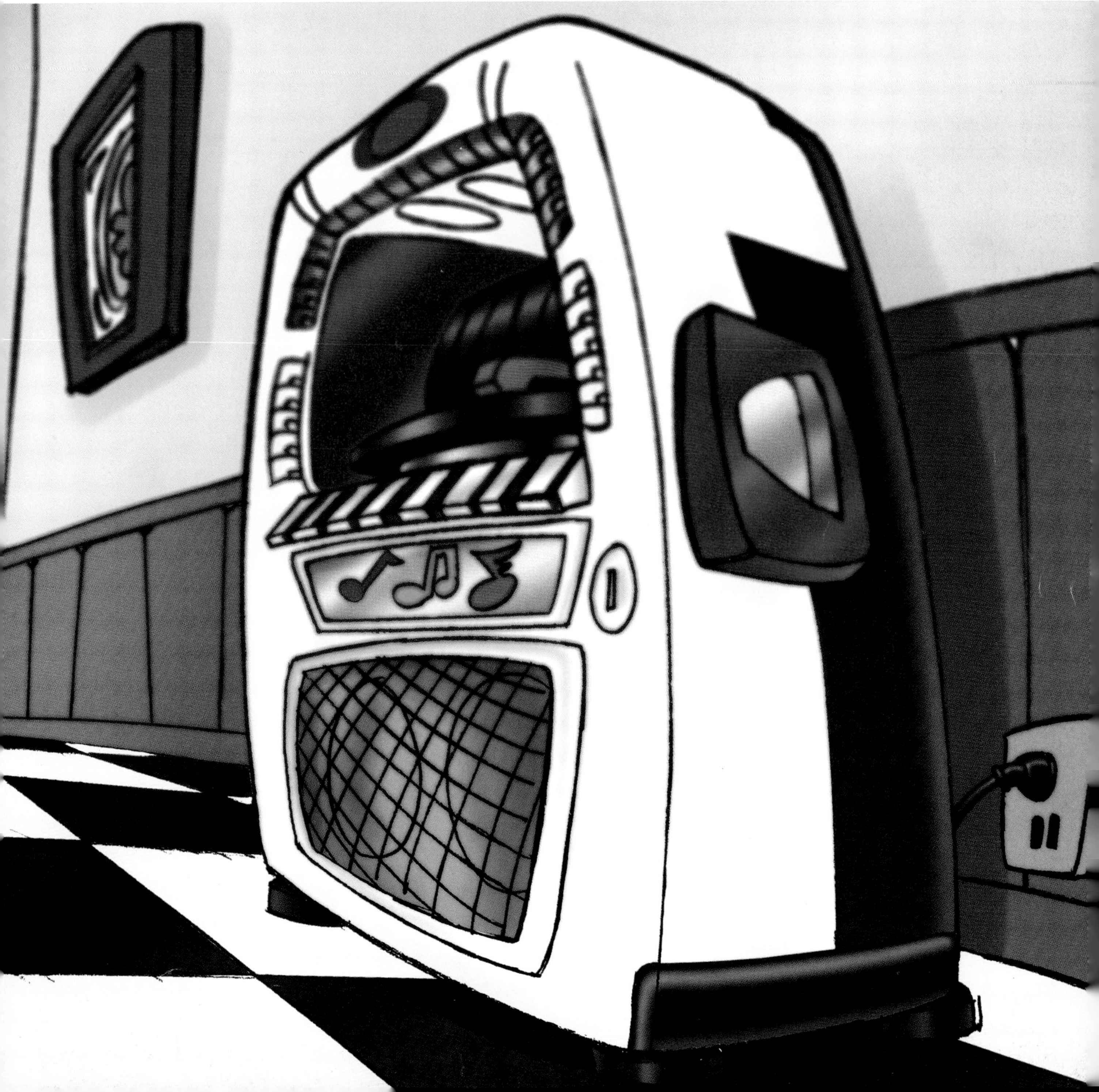

See, anyone can do the limbo.

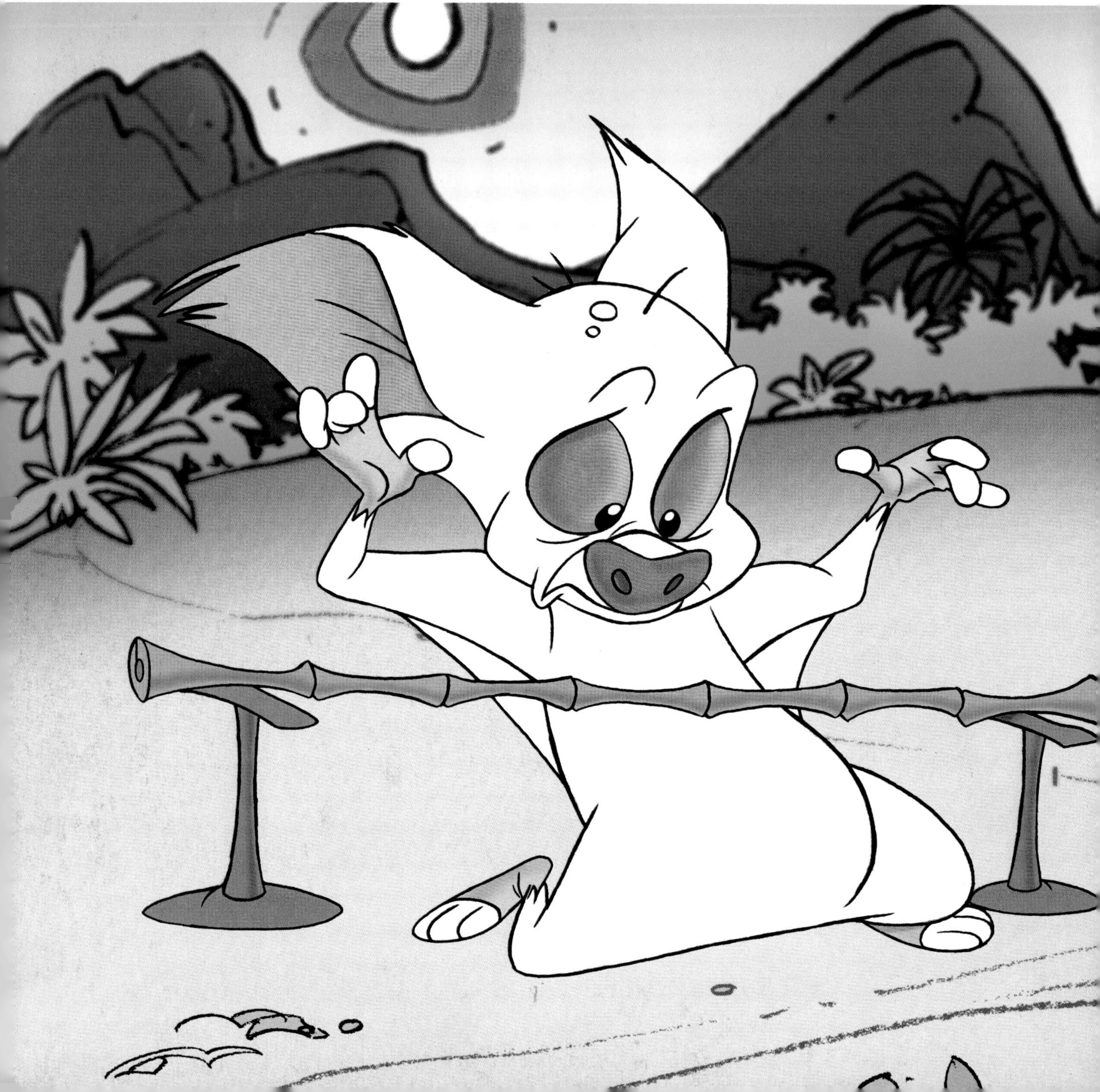

Crouch down low and go, go, go!

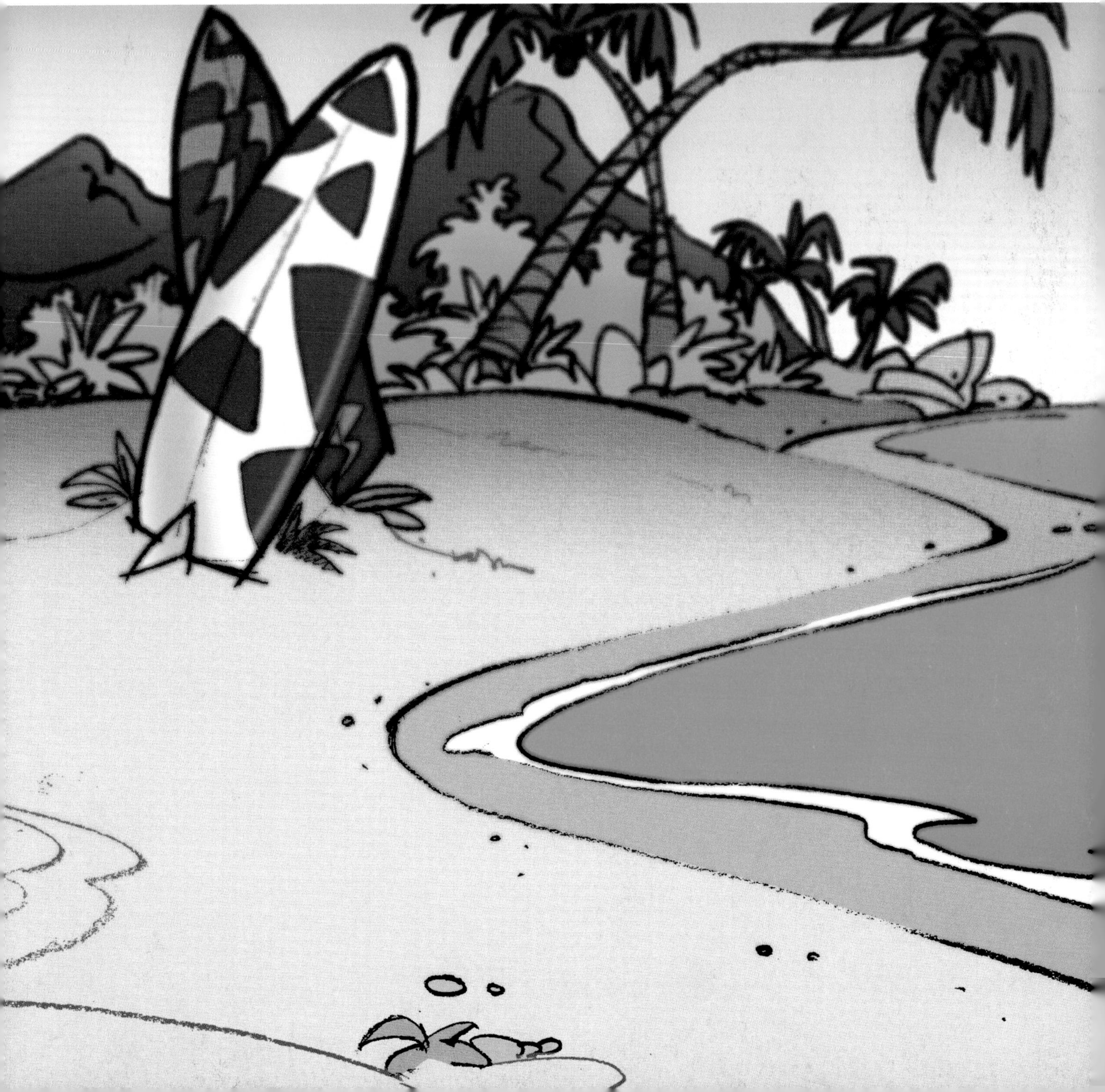

And if you learn to do the hula,

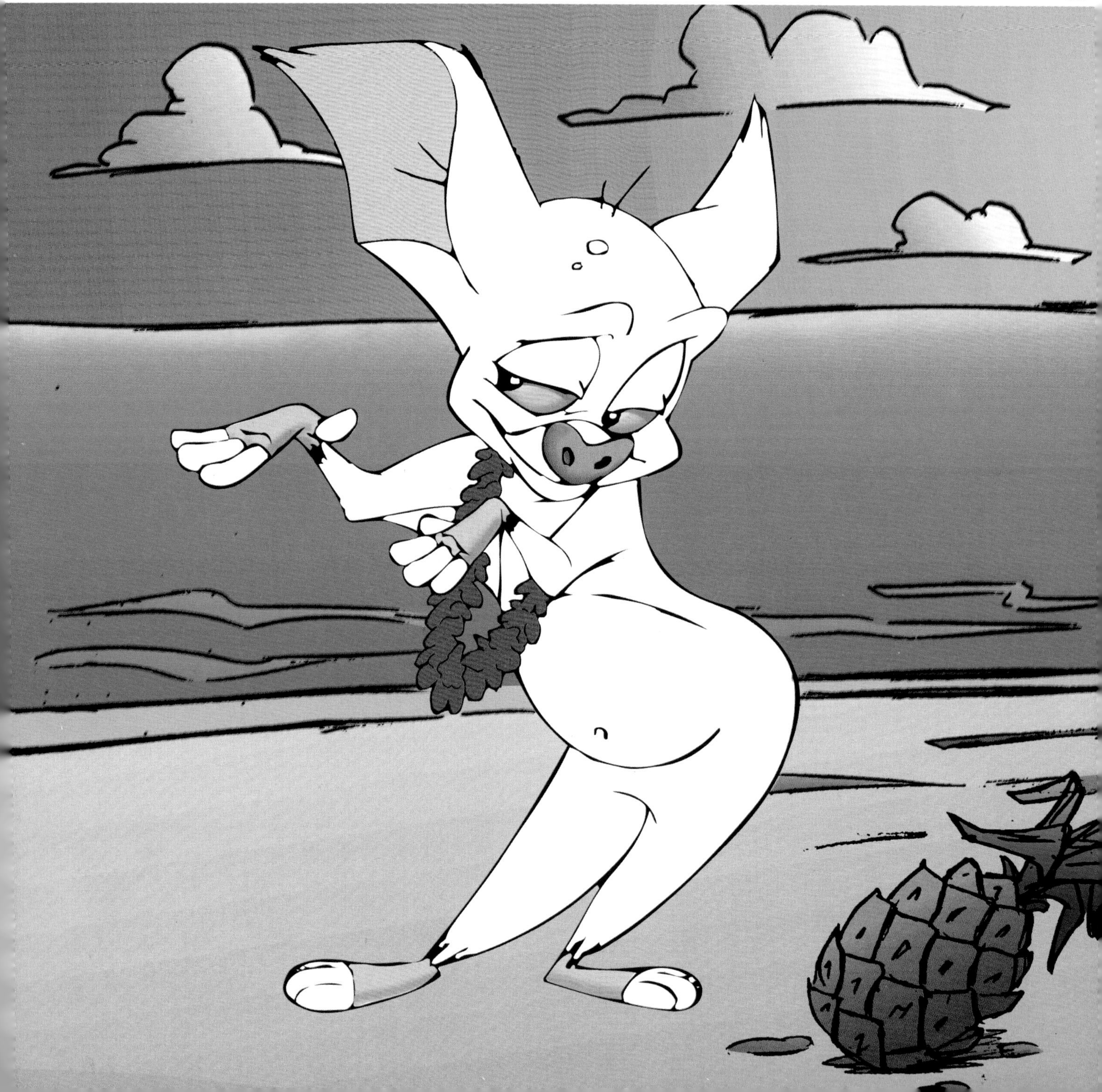

you could make some serious moola!

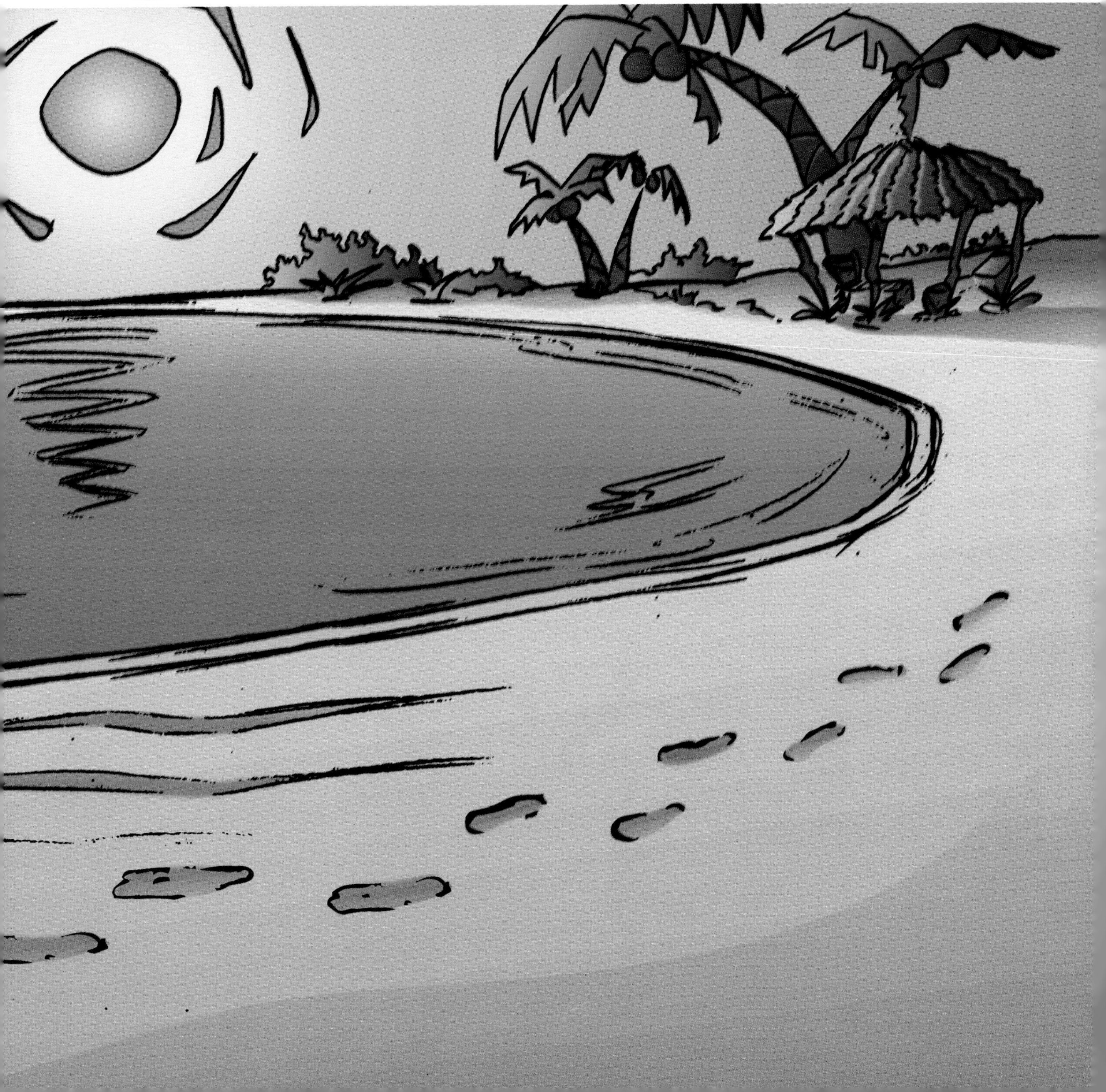

Ballet requires a certain flair.

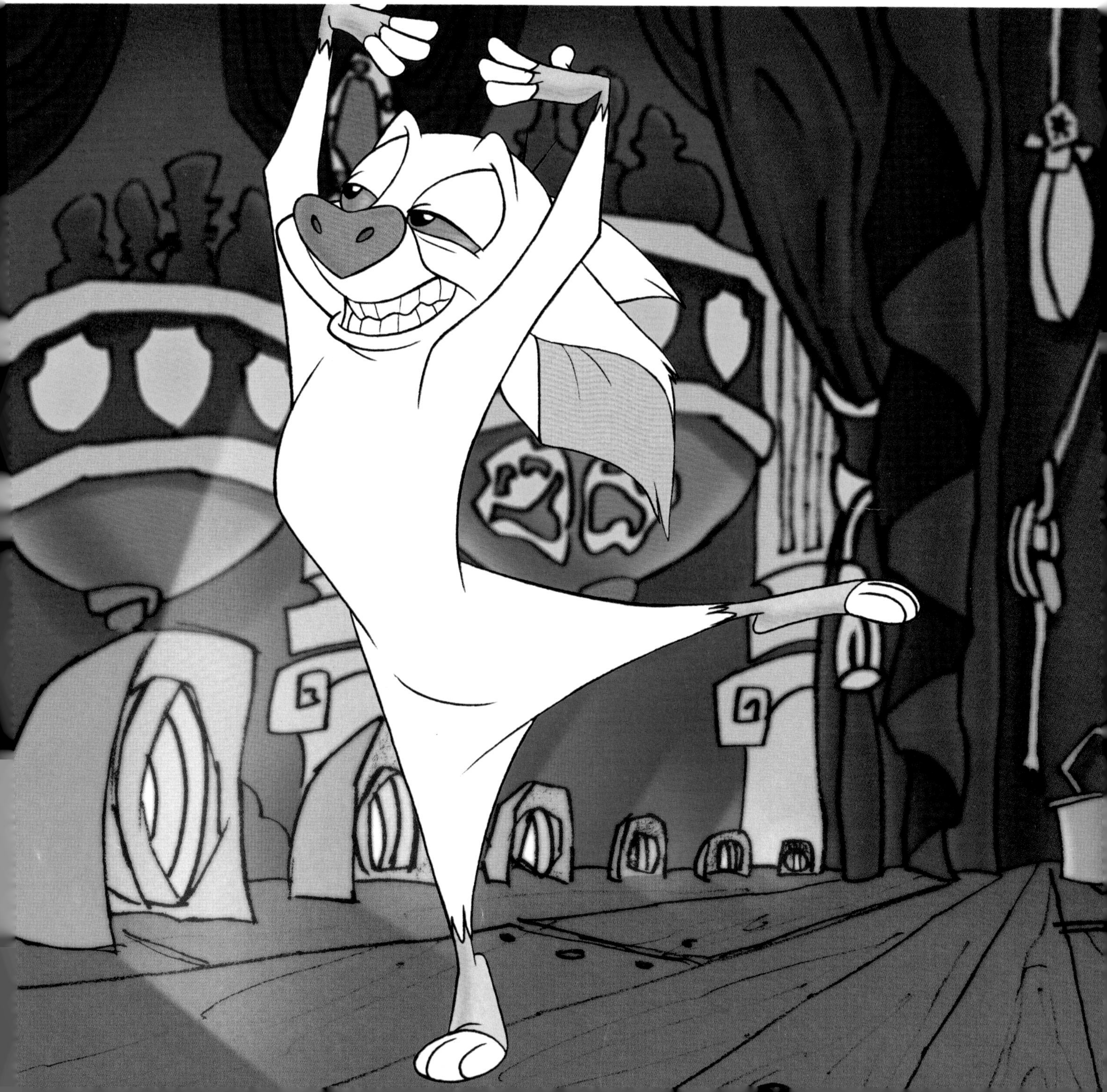

When you're not on your toes, you're in the air!

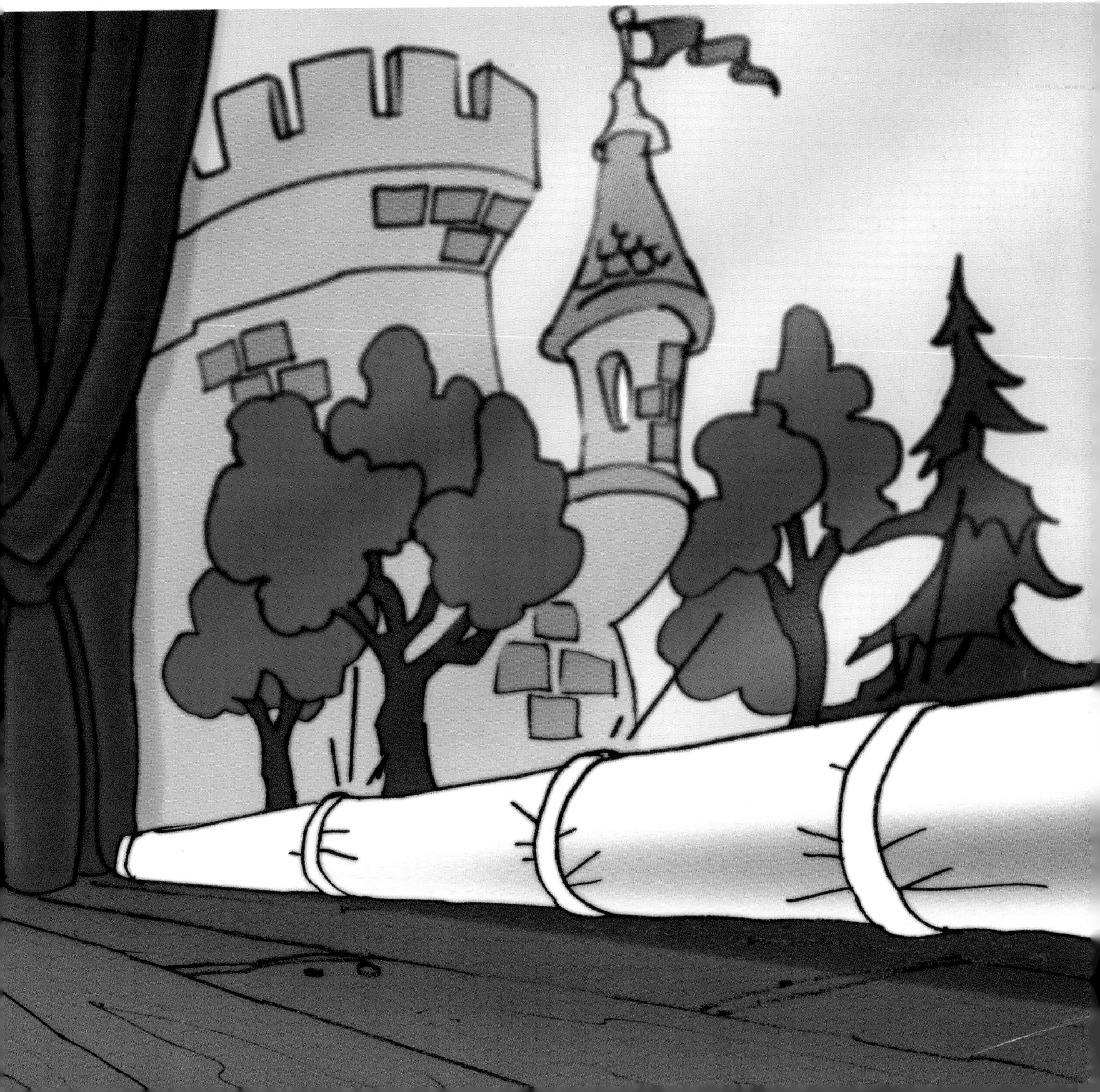

The last step I'll show you is the best of all.

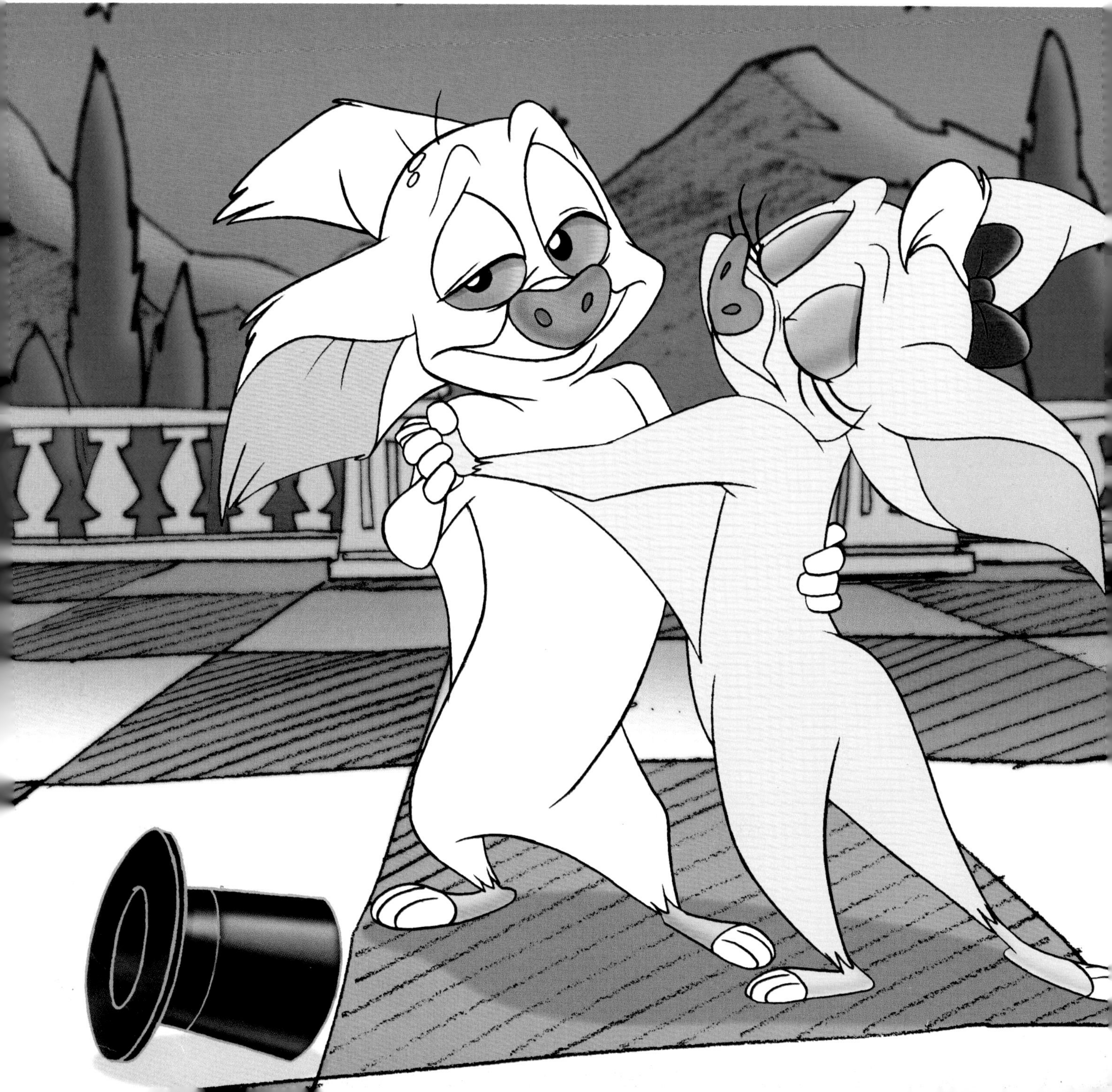

You dip your partner, but don't let her fall!

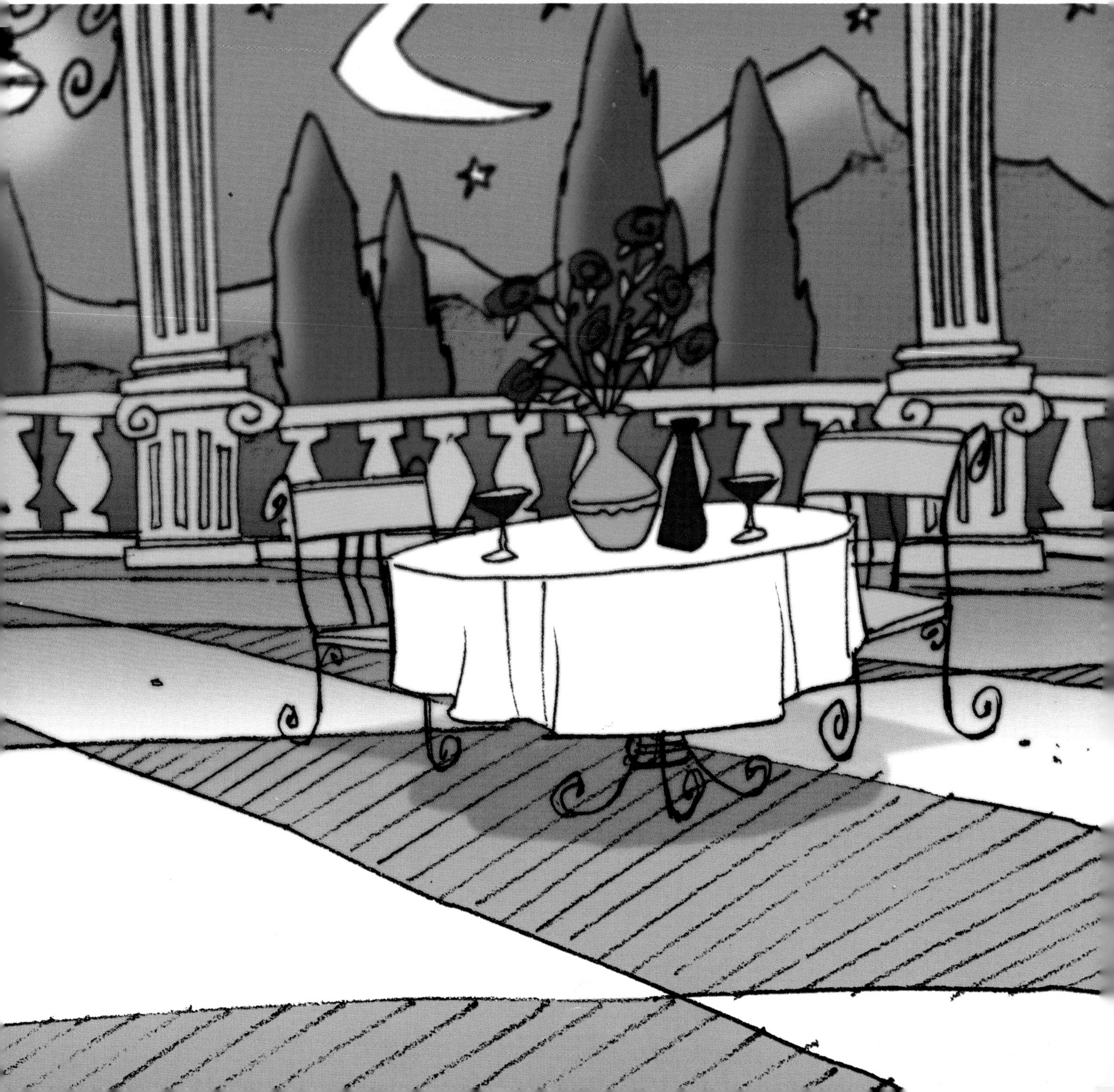

Rasputin here may be my master,

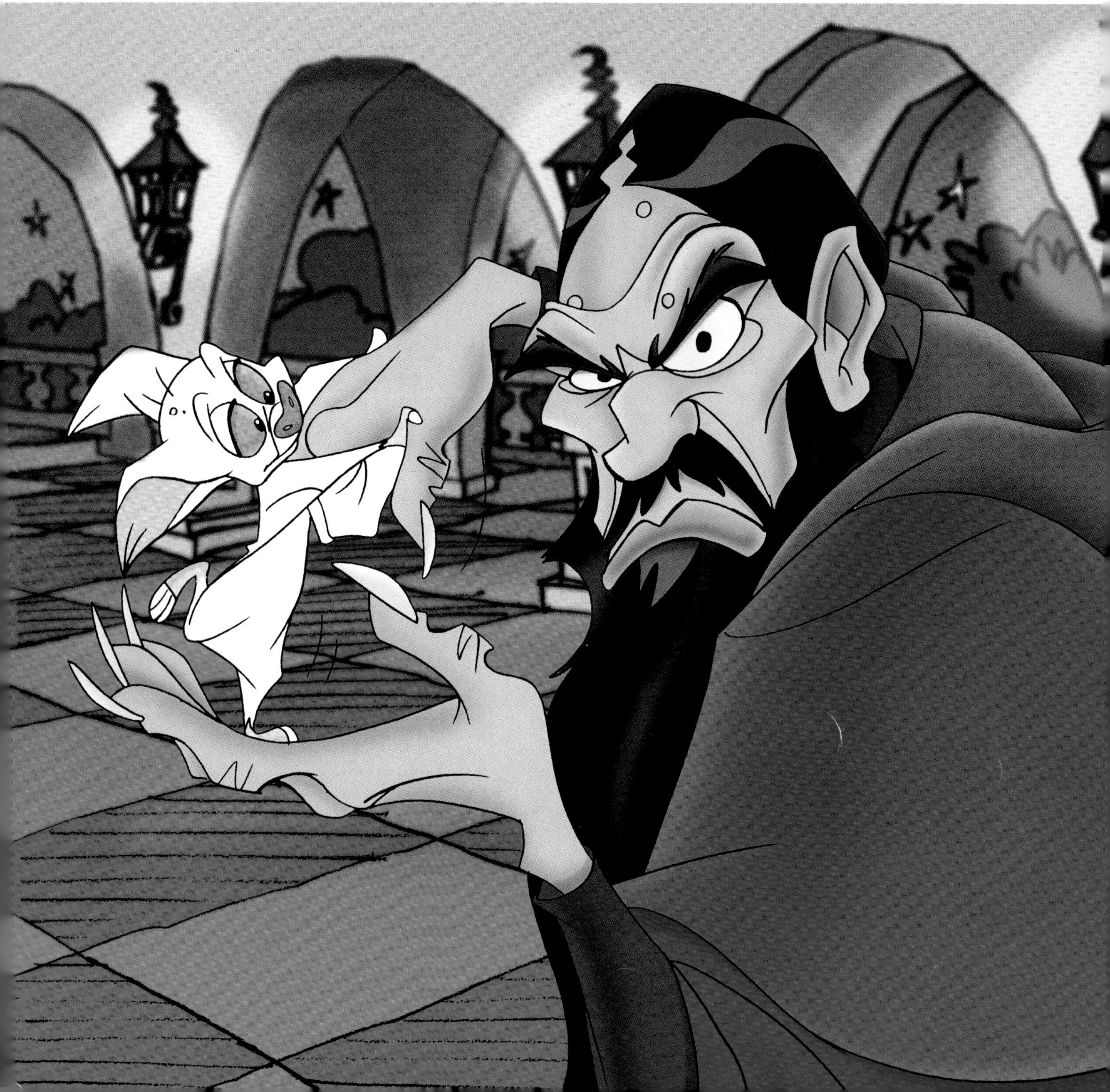

but on the dance floor he's one *big* disaster.

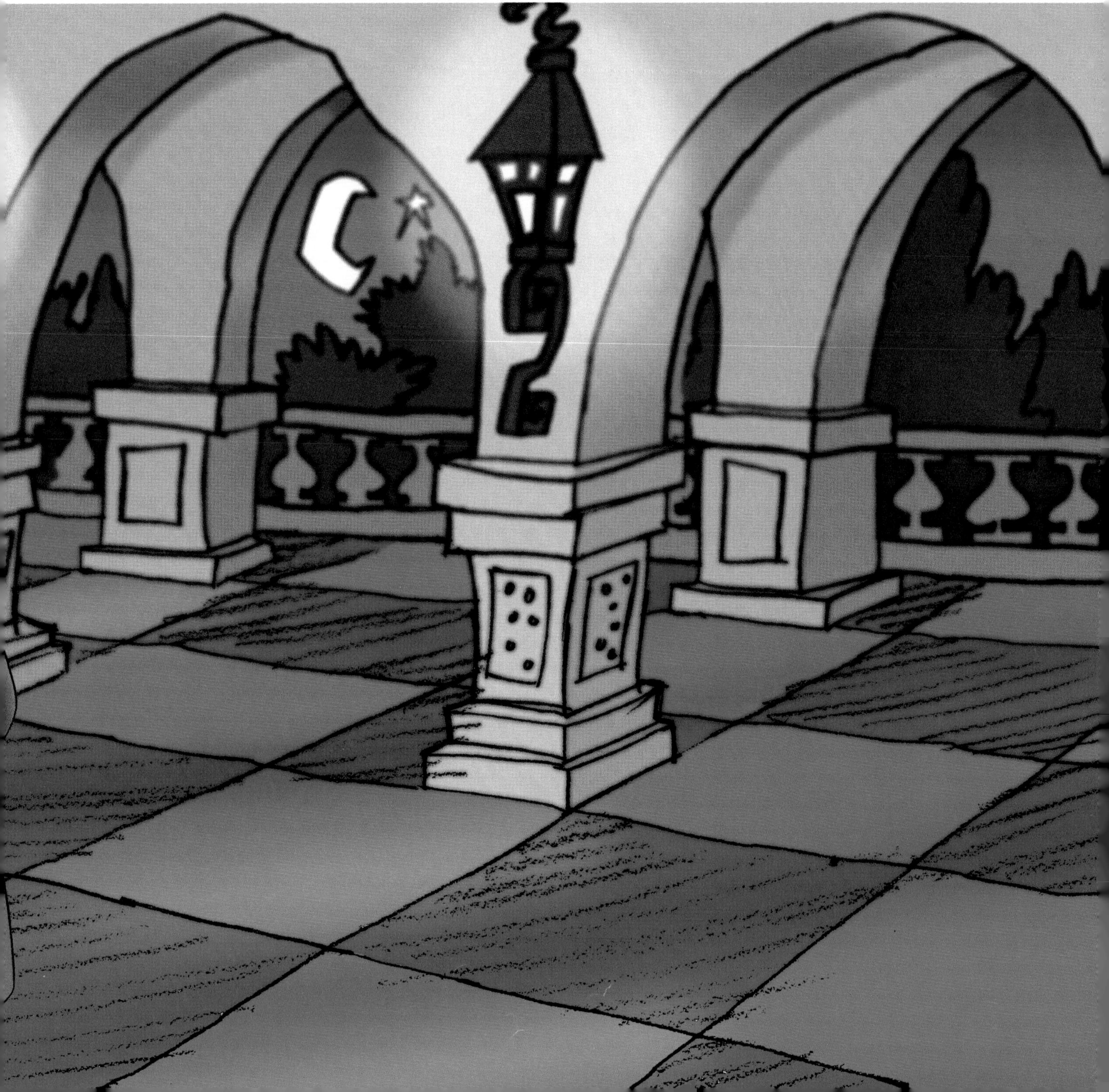

You, on the other hand, are quite the smarty.

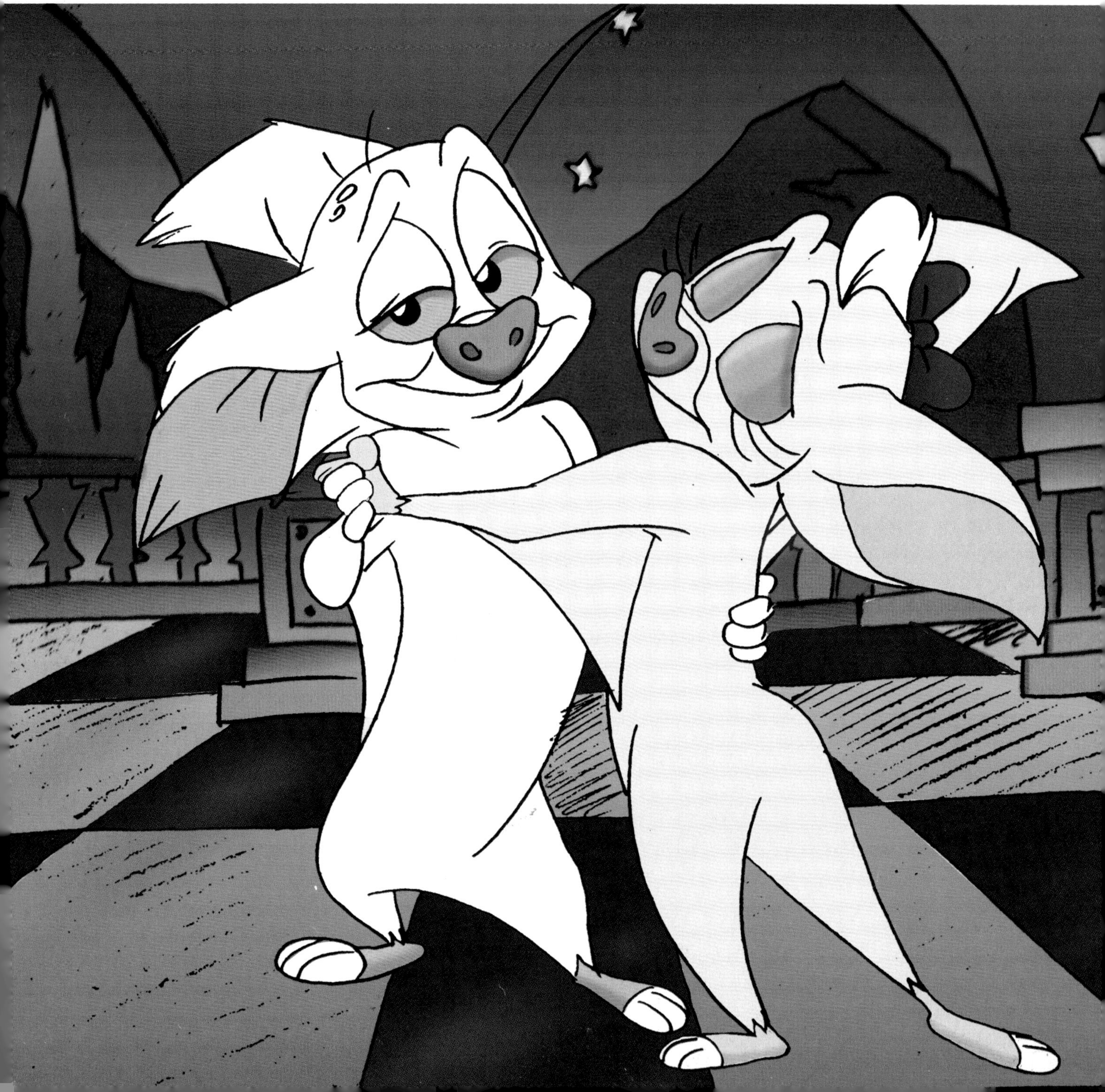

You learned to dance. Now you're the life of the party!

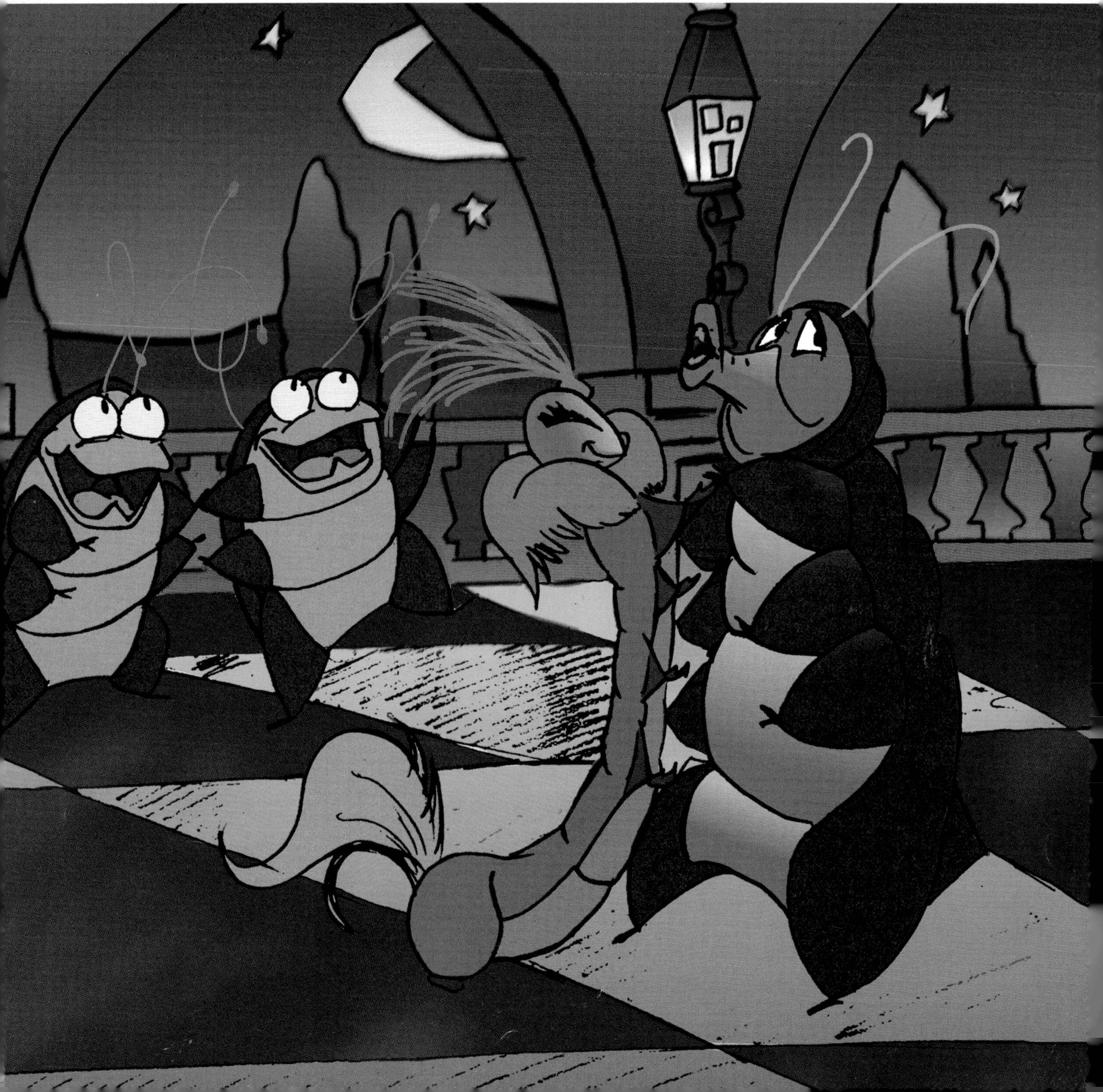

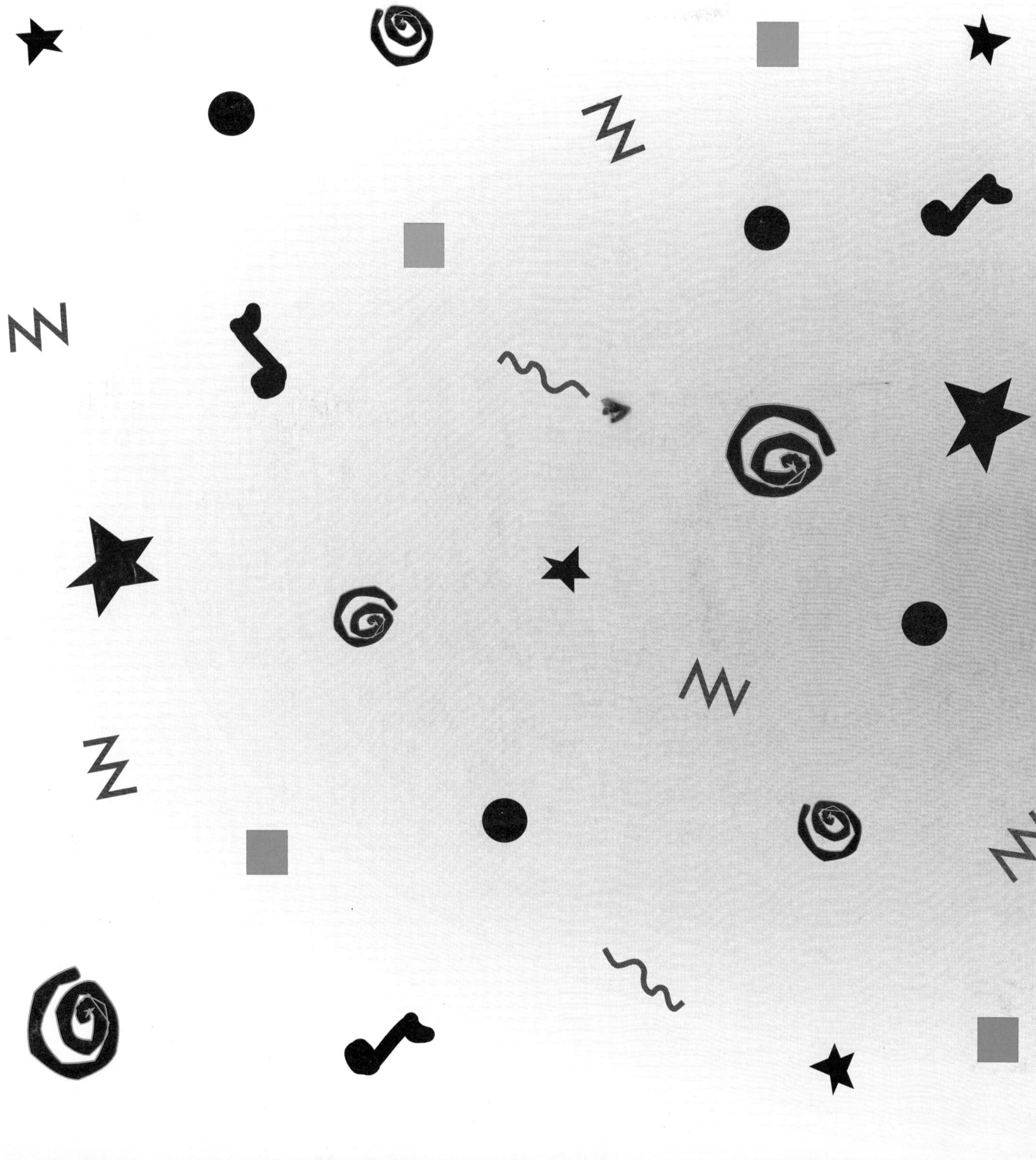